VISIONS OF MURDER

MEGAN VAZ

This book is dedicated to my Parents & Grandmother, who constantly remind me that I can do anything I put my mind to.

Also, to their immense faith and support in me. It is also dedicated to my friends who have helped me create some of these storylines and edited them.

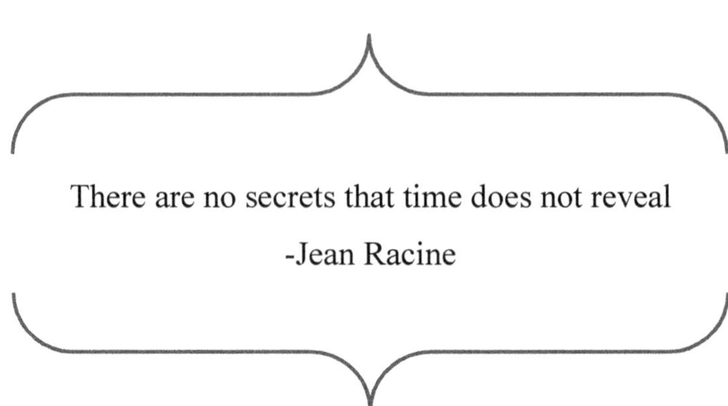
There are no secrets that time does not reveal
-Jean Racine

Prologue

The final murder was the one that made the clocks stop. The snow crunched underfoot as the killer dragged the last body into the woods. The bloody knife slipped from their grip, clattering against the cabin steps, sounding like a China plate being smashed. The water turned red as the blood from the knife swirled down the drain. The nervousness and anxious feeling began to take over. Had someone seen or heard the noises? Were the cops on their way up? Did I still have a conscience? "If only the walls had ears," he said.

A shiver went down my spine as I cleaned the mess in the Cabin. Why couldn't it be simple? All I ever asked for was the truth. The dark side, which I had warned everyone about, had now prevailed. It wasn't like I wanted this, but they needed to be taught a lesson. They took me for a fool for far too long, and now they had to pay the price with their lives.

I went back out into the forest. I burned it all. Now, only the forest and I knew the secret that happened on that fateful day on a sugar bush trip that went oh so wrong.

Hello,

I hope prison hasn't been too rough. I made arrangements for you to have your very own cell and be protected. I am sorry that this is what it had to come to, but I knew it was for the best. I am sure your time hasn't been easy. You probably have many questions burning within you. As do I. I wish I could fix it all but the only thing I can do is explain and hope that you will understand the course of actions that caused this. For what it is worth, I forgive you.

Chapter 1

My eyes shot open only to be blinded by a light; my head was pounding, and I couldn't figure out where I was until I looked down to see an IV sticking out of my arm. I started pulling it out, along with the other cords attached to my body, triggering the alarm on the monitor. Three nurses ran into my room, trying to put me back in bed and yelling, "Please, ma'am, you've been in an accident; you're in a hospital! Please stop!"

It was like a scene from a hospital drama show where the patient is trying to leave, and a nurse or doctor is trying to persuade them not to. Finally, one of the nurses who was not pulling me to get back into bed turned off the monitor, catching me off guard and making me freeze. She told the other nurses to back away, pulled up a chair, and sat down.

"My name is Helen. I am the head nurse here at Memorial General Hospital. I know that you're scared, but I am here to help you." Helen was an older lady, maybe in her 40s, with a bun that sat perfectly at the top of her head, and she had green cat-like eyes. She wore librarian-type glasses, the bold-looking ones, and had on Lion King Scrubs. She spoke very softly and calmly, "Can I get you anything? Some water? Painkillers?"

"No!" I exclaimed. "I…I just want to know why I'm here and what happened!"

"You don't remember anything?" Helen asked, sounding concerned.

"No."

Helen just sighed and shook her head. "What? What is it?" I asked.

"I was afraid of that," Helen said. She pulled her chair closer to me as if she wanted no one else to hear.

"Ms. Clarke," she began, "Bailey. Please call me Bailey," I interrupt, "Okay, Bailey… you were brought in with serious head trauma. You lost a significant amount of blood and have been in a coma for three days. We were all really worried about you. It seems like you hit your head with a lot of force. Do you remember how it happened?"

"No, I don-…" and just then I remembered something.

It was dark; I was running away from something, no – SOMEONE! As I ran, I could hear the snow crunching underneath me as well as from behind me, as if someone was chasing after me. Then it all went black. "Bailey? Sweetheart? Are you okay?" Helen asked, bringing me back from my flashback.

"Yes! I remember running away from someone, then slipping on ice."

"Why were you running? Who was chasing you?" Helen asked softly.

"I don't remember anymore," I said as I held my head to try and ease the pounding feeling. Helen must have noticed my pain because she stood and held my face in her hands, and with a smile, she said, "I'll be back with some painkillers and soup."

"Thank you," I said sheepishly. "Helen?" "Yes, dear?"

"How did I get here? Who found me?"

"A man brought you in. He's right there." She pointed to a man, curled up on a chair, sound asleep. I couldn't make out what he looked like, so I asked her if she could d send him in. She nodded and said, "Of course, he'll be glad to know you're finally awake. He hasn't left since he brought you in. And off the record, he's cute." We both laughed, and she left the room.

As I lay in bed, I remembered that my fiancé, our friends, and I had been on a road trip to a sugar bush. I started to wonder where they were, but before panic could set in again, there was a knock at the door. "Come in", I said. It was him. The man who had saved my life. He was tall with a brownish face. He had black hair with mini wave-like curls like waves, dark brown eyes, and a skinny build. He had an un-explanatory boyish charm to him. I scanned him up and down, trying to get a gauge of who he was.

"Bailey, isn't it?" His voice was deep but not too deep. "Yes, please sit," I said, gesturing to the chair.

"No thanks," he said, moving to lean against the wall, "I am glad to see you are safe."

"Thanks to you," I said and smiled. He just looked at me with a blank face and hummed before saying, "Well, I hope it wasn't a mistake." I gave him a puzzled look, hoping he would explain, but he just walked out. "Please wait! At least tell me your name."

"Ethan," he replied without turning around, and then he just vanished down the corridor.

At the same time, Helen came back with the medication and soup. "Here you go," she smiled as she handed me the medication. "Now finish your soup and try to get some sleep; hopefully, you will remember some more in the morning."

"Thank you, Helen; I hope so too."

"HELP! HELP! Is anyone out there? Please! If you can hear me, please help me!" I looked down at my hands to see them covered in blood.

"Ms. Clarke? Bailey? Bailey, wake up!"

I sit up abruptly, my arm shooting out and grabbing the first thing it touches. "Helen?!" I said as I grabbed her tightly and hugged her.

"Are you alright? You were having a nightmare," she says softly.

"No. But I think I'm remembering more. I can see a dark forest, snow, and blood."

"Blood!?" she gasps as she pulls out of the hug a little to look into my eyes.

"Yeah, it is all so weird."

"You're telling me," She chuckles nervously. "Anyway, I will be right back with your breakfast."

"Okay," I said, lying back down as she left.

"Oh, I almost forgot to give this to you, someone left this note at the nurses' station."

"Do you know who left it?" I asked as I slowly took it from her.

"Unfortunately, no, no one saw. It was just sitting there with your name on it."

"Oh, thank you."

"You're welcome; I will be right back," and with that, she left the room.

I stared at the letter, the writing did not look familiar, nor could I think of anyone who would have left it. I opened it up and enclosed was a key necklace and a note that said… "Meet me at 10 pm tonight at *Asher's Bay Cabins, 1420 Derry Road. Cabin 7..* I was confused and scared, but something deep inside me felt like this could bring me closer to the answers I needed. I heard Helen's heels approaching my room, so I quickly shoved the letter under the blankets. "Here you go, sweetie," she said, placing the tray down.

"Thank you. Helen, do you know when I can leave?"

"I wouldn't recommend it anytime soon, but I suppose if you really wanted to leave, you could at any time," she stated.

"Okay, in that case, can I have the release papers?"

"As you wish," she replied. And with that, she left to get them. I went to change into my old clothes, but as I laid them out, I noticed they were stained with blood. Just then, Helen came back with the papers and some clean clothes. "I remembered that your clothes wouldn't be the best to wear, so I gathered some from the

Lost & Found bin. They seem to be about your size," she said with a smile, "and here are the papers; just sign them and leave them on the bed. Here is my number; if you ever need me or anything, please do not hesitate to call."

"Thank you, Helen, for everything," I said as I hugged her.

I quickly changed into the clothes she had laid out, signed the documents, packed my old clothes into my bag, and left.

Chapter 2

"Asher's Bay Cabins, 1420 Derry Road," I said to the taxi driver. He was an older man, maybe in his 60's, and with a Jersey accent, he said: "Miss, that's a three-hour drive out of the city!"

"I know; just get me there, please."

"Alright," he said and started the car, "so why are you heading up there?"

"I have a meeting with someone."

"Oooo… a secret rendezvous of sorts?" he asked with a sexual undertone.

"Um… no. More like an 'I have no idea what this is about' kind of meeting," I said. We made eye contact in the rearview mirror, his eyes showing concern for me, almost like he was hoping I would tell him to turn around, but instead, I just nuzzled my head into the seat and fell asleep.

"Please! Somebody?! Anybody?! Help Me?!"— "Miss? Miss!"

"What?! What?!" I yelled as I jumped up in my seat, nearly hitting my head on the roof.

"We're here." The taxi driver said, "It looks like no one has been here in ages; there isn't a single car. Are you sure about this?" He asked.

"I have to," I replied, gathering my stuff.

"Right. Can I at least wait here for you, just to make sure you are okay?"

"Thank you, sir, but there is really no need," I said as I handed him the money. "No, no, please keep your money. All I ask is that you stay safe."

"Thank you," I said, and I climbed out of the cab.

I heard him pull out as I stared at this cabin in the woods situation. I could hear a lake somewhere behind me. I took a deep breath of fresh air.

"Okay. You can do this", I said, hyping myself up, and then started to walk. "Cabin 7, cabin 7, cabin 7…" I finally came to a door with a brass metal 7 on it. The light was on, which meant whoever had asked me to meet them here was waiting for me. I put the key in and turned the knob. As I walked inside, I could hear a shower running.

"Hello? It's me, Bailey. I got your note." The shower stopped.

I turned around to close the door, and from behind me, I heard, "I'm glad you made it." The voice sounded familiar, so I turned around quickly to see Ethan wrapped in a towel.

"Ethan?" I gasped.

"The one and only," he said laughing.

"Wha- What is all this? Why did you bring me here? Who are you?" I asked, my anger and confusion seeping into my tone, and I stepped towards him with each question.

"Whoa, whoa, whoa…relax. Sit down." He said as he grabbed my shoulders and pushed me down on to the couch. He sat on a chair across from me and began to answer my questions.

"I'm Ethan..." he started, and I interrupted him by saying, "Well, no, duh." and rolling my eyes. He just giggled and said, "That's the Bailey I know." I looked at him, baffled.

"I am guessing you still do not remember a lot from that night. I also cannot exactly tell you; you have to try and remember it all." He got up and moved closer to me, pushing my hair out of my face; he asked, "Do you know why I chose this place or who I am?"

"No, I'm sorry, I really don't, I wis-" I started to say before he jumped in.

"Shhh...It is fine. Maybe this will help jog your memory," he whispered and then kissed me ever so gently on my lips.

"I still don't remember, but don't stop," I whispered back while pulling him closer to me. He stood up, lifted me gently, and laid me down on the bed, his lips moving from my neck back up to mine in a trail of kisses. He pulled away but stayed just close enough for me to beg him to continue. His eyes searched mine as if silently asking for permission. I smiled and nodded, giving him the answer he needed. Something about this felt normal, almost like I had known him all my life. He suddenly touched my side, making me flinch. He quickly pulled his hand away, looking apologetic. He started to apologize, but I shushed him and lifted my shirt to see what had caused that sudden pain. There was a bandage. I removed to see what looked like a stab wound. The night passed, and we fell asleep, holding each other 'BANG! BANG! BANG!' I woke with a start, startled by the pounding at my door.

"Ethan! Ethan! I think someone is at the door. Ethan?" but there was no sound or sign of him. "Ms. Clarke, this is the police. Open the door..." Someone yelled through the door. "One moment, please; I'm coming." I draped a blanket over myself and went to the door, still confused about why the cops were there and where Ethan had gone. As I got to the door, I noticed there was another note that read, "I'm sorry. –Ethan." I crumpled the note into my pocket and opened the door.

"Ms. Clarke?" the policeman asked. "Yes, that's me, officer."

"I'm afraid you are under arrest." - "ARREST?!" - "Please turn around." He handcuffed me and then walked me to his cruiser. He read me my rights as I calculated every possible outcome that could have brought me to this place. Once we reached the police station, they placed me in an interrogation room, where I just sat, trying to piece together everything from start to finish, but I just couldn't.

"Do you know why you are here, Ms. Clarke?" the officer asked me.

"No officer, I don't," I replied. He looked at me as if he didn't know whether to believe me or lock me up right here and now. He sighed and pulled out a folder. He placed pictures in front of me, and with each photo, I could feel my stomach twisting and turning as the nauseating feeling increased. The photos were horrific and depicted gruesome murders.

"This young man had his head bashed in. This young lady had her throat slit, and this one was stabbed 7 times," the officer said, pointing to each picture.

"What do these pictures have to do with me?" I asked, fearing the answer.

"Look closer. Can you tell me who they are?" he asked. I lifted the picture closest to me and brought it closer to my face. I saw a tattoo, a tattoo that only one man in my life had, and that man was my fiancé.

"No! NO! Tell me it's not true." I screamed as tears began to fill my eyes. The officer looked at me, finally seeing how devastated I was, and suddenly softened his tone as he said: "Three of your friends were found dead near the sugar bush a couple of days ago. We don't know what happened and the only person to have regained consciousness was you.

The only way we know who you are was because we found your engagement ring a few miles from the murder scene." "Officer…" I started.

"Sam. Call me Sam," he said.

"Okay, Sam. I really can't help you; I don't know what happened. I woke up in a hospital room, and that's all I can remember." I told him, hoping the questions would stop.

"How did you end up in the hospital?" Sam asked, ignoring my silent plea.

"A man by the name of Ethan. I-I don't know his last name, but he brought me there. You can even confirm my story with my nurse, Helen." I said.

"I do find it odd that you were in the same place where they were murdered." He stated, sounding skeptical.

"Look, I got a note from someone telling me to meet them there, and I went. Seriously, go confirm my story with Helen." I insisted. "I will, until then, do not leave town, and I suggest you find yourself a hell of a good lawyer." "Does that mean I am free to go?"

"For now," he said dryly. I got up to leave, but then I remembered something Sam said, and it prompted me to ask, "Sam, you said that three of my friends were found dead. However, there were 5 of us. Then you said I was the only one to have regained consciousness. Is someone still alive?"

Sam turned to me and said, "We don't know his name yet. He has black hair, and..." but before he could finish his sentence, I yelled, "Dustin!"

Sam shot up. "Is that his name?" he asked. "Yes. Can I see him?" I begged.

"Unfortunately, no. He is in critical condition, and as this is an ongoing investigation, it will just be safer for the both of you to stay apart until this is all over." I wasn't happy with his answer, but I nodded and left. As I walked down the steps from the station to get to the bus stop, Sam came running out.

"Ms. Clarke, I'm not supposed to say this, but, in a way, you seem kind of nice. My friend owns a Bed and Breakfast motel a little way from here. 187 Chestnut Drive. I think it will be decent a place for you to stay while this case is in progress." I thanked him for his suggestion, called a taxi, and went on my way.

I asked the taxi to make a stop back at the cabin. I had hoped that Ethan would be there, but he wasn't. I accepted that this man was never going to come back and besides, I had other things to worry about. My freedom was on the line. So, we continued to the bed and breakfast motel.

When I got to the bed and breakfast, I went to the main office only to notice that no one was there. As I went to ring the little bell, a pretty girl popped up from behind the counter. "Welcome to Nancy and George's Bed and Breakfast!" she said jovially.

"You must be Nancy?" I asked.

"No, although I get that a lot. I'm actually their daughter, Mary-Ellen. Do you need a room? And for how long?" she asked.

"Indefinitely," I replied. "Sure, I can pull that for you. You're in luck; you missed the car show rush. We were all sold out."

I just gave her a half-moon smile as she continued. "Can I get a name for the room?"

"Uh…yeah, it's Bailey Clarke."

"Bailey Clarke! Why didn't you say that before? No need for anything. Your room is all set up. Room 17."

"Excuse me?" I asked hesitantly.

"Sam called me earlier telling me you would be needing a room. He said he would take care of everything. He's a sweetheart like that," she smiled, glancing at a picture on the counter of the two of them hugging.

"No, I can't have him…" I started to say, but before I could finish my sentence, she cut me off, saying, "Well, you will have to take that up with him. All I know is I am not going against our top officer."

"Alright then." She grabbed the key from the wall and handed it to me, saying, "Take the steps on your left, and the room will be at the end of the hall." I thanked her and left. When I got to the room, I settled in, but something was pressing me to go to the hospital to see with my own eyes if it really was Dustin. So, I called for a cab and headed back to where I woke up.

Chapter 3

When I got to the hospital I went straight for the Nurse's station. The Nurse there didn't look up but asked who I was there to see. "Dustin Murray."

"Are you a family member?" she asked. "No, I am a close friend of his," I replied.

"Only family is allowed to see him," she said sternly. I started to walk away until I saw a cluster of people. I hopped in with them and tried to hide. After passing the nurse, I parted from the group and went on my own to find him; after all, how hard could it be? I followed to sign to the ICU section of the hospital. Surprisingly, there was no one around, so I made my way to the computer behind the nurses' station and went to patient lookup. It looks like my hacking skills paid off. The computer was lagging a bit but eventually, it allowed me to type in his name. **Dustin Murray; Room 106: NO VISTORS ALLOWED- Officer Sam Carter.**

Well, what officer Sam doesn't know won't kill him. I started to hear indistinct chattering, so I quickly jotted down the information on a sticky note, then cleared the computer and left.

I walked the halls, looking at the numbers until I came to his room. The door was closed, and the blinds were sealed shut. No one was around. I could feel the butterflies in my stomach as I reached for the door handle. I pressed down, took a deep breath, and walked in. I closed the door ever so silently and then turned around to see my best friend lying lifelessly on a hospital bed.

"Dustin," I gasped in a whisper. I moved closer to him, feeling tears welling up in my eyes. Noticing a clipboard hanging at the foot of the bed, I picked it up and began reviewing the pages. My attention was drawn to the section detailing his injuries.

Injuries: gunshot wound to the shoulder; no major arteries hit. 3 stab wounds to the lower abdomen. Lost lots of Blood. "I don't understand what brought us here." I pulled the chair from the corner and sat down, then grabbed his hand in mine. "You don't deserve this. None of you did. I wish I could take it all back. You need to wake up and come back to me. I can't do it without you!" I begged and cried. Then I took off my shoes and crawled up beside him in the bed. His breathing soothed my jitters. I just laid next to him, eyes closed. After a little while, I felt a squeeze on my hand. Startled, I open my eyes and look at him. I could see no signs of him walking out of his coma, but I could hear footsteps approaching. I jumped off the bed, put my shoes on, and put my hood over my head.

As I opened the door, so did the nurse. We both gave each other a startle, and she said, "You aren't supposed to be in here," as she grabbed my arm. I pulled out of her grip and began to walk fast down the corridor. She was still yelling about how she was calling the police and security, so I began to run with my head down. I hopped into the elevator and went all the way to the first level. I rushed out of the elevator and bumped into someone. The person grabbed my shoulders and said, "Whoa, someone is in a rush. Are you okay?" My eyes just widened. The voice was as familiar as the shadow that followed you in the light. I nodded abruptly and headed for the door without looking back.

Chapter 4

I got back to the motel and sat on the bed trying to make sense of what had happened today and tried to replay everything in my head. Maybe if I got some sleep, I thought to myself, my subconscious would prove helpful.

"Babe, take a left here." "You sure, Bailey?" "Yes... I remember."

"That was so much fun! I definitely think I ate too much maple taffy, hahaha…" Dustin laughed.

"No, I think James here has you beat," I joked, lightly smacking him.

"Yeah…look at his fingers. They are already sticking together," Cynthia chimed in.

"Let's turn on some music," Alina said. I plugged my phone into the aux, and we shuffled through songs until we found the perfect one. We continued driving, but it was getting late, and I could feel James getting more anxious, so he started to speed up.

"James, hun, you might want to slow down, we are still on dirt roads."

"No, it will be fine; this car can handle it," he replied.

"I really think you should slow down; there is a curve coming up," I said. Earlier in the day, I had convinced everyone to take an impromptu road trip. So, the five of us decided to take a day trip to the sugar bush factory.

Next thing we know, we hit a bump in the road, and then Bang! The bottom of the car hits the dirt. Dustin, Cynthia, and Alina, who had fallen asleep, woke in a panic. I look at James with an 'I told you so' look, but before the words come out of my mouth, he turns to me and says, "Don't say it." James and Dustin got out of the car to try and see if anything was damaged. "Shit!" The girls and I looked at each other and then got out of the car.

"What's wrong?" Alina inquired.

"James over here damaged the shocks," Dustin stated. "So, what does that exactly mean for us?" I asked James.

"Means we can't drive back because the highway will destroy my car. So, we have to call CAA and wait it out."

"Great!" Cynthia huffed, annoyed. "Well, instead of freezing out here, let's get back into the car and call', Alina suggested. So that's what we did. James called while the rest of us just sat there.

"They don't know exactly how long it will take since there is a storm headed our way," said James.

"Maybe we could walk back to the sugar factory? We aren't too far, and it beats sitting in the middle of nowhere," Alina said.

We all agreed that would beat sitting in the car, so we grabbed our bags and sct out.

20 minutes into our walk, the cold started to hit. It was as cold and as bitter as the Siberian winter weather front sweeping across Europe, dragging the temperature records down to a record low. When they warned me about the Innisfree winters, no one did a good job. You could feel the cold penetrate your skin. How much longer?" Alina chattered out, crossing her arms over her chest.

"I think it's only a few more kilometers," Dustin said, glasses fogged. After what seemed like another 3 hours of walking in the killer cold, we reached "*INISFREE'S SUGARBUSH*."

"Finally!" James exclaimed. Just behind the sugar mill, we saw little cabins. The only decent and non-Texas chainsaw-looking one was cabin 7. As we walked towards it, we saw the sign: *Asher's Bay Cabins, 1420 Derry Road. Cabin 7*. We could hear the lake behind it.

"Doesn't look like anyone is here, though, so great idea," Cynthia said sarcastically, turning to look at me.

"It was Alina's plan," I said sharply. Cynthia just shook her head and walked away. Ever since James and I started dating,

Cynthia and I have never seen eye to eye, and it only got worse once we got engaged. I rolled my eyes as we began to climb the steps of the cabin. We reached the front door and, out of courtesy, knocked, but there was no answer.

"I'm gonna go check the back. Dustin, come with me? I'll prop you up," James said as he started towards the back of the cabin. "Sure," Dustin replied, following James.

While they went to check the back, I told the girls, "Maybe we could find a spare key under something." Alina agreed, so we started to lift and move anything we could.

"This would go a lot faster if you helped, you know Cynthia," I said, my tone doing nothing to hide how annoyed I was. She just sighed and got down on her knees to help.

A few minutes later, Cynthia exclaimed, "Found it!" while holding it up high as if she were holding the Holy Grail.

"Great job, Cynthia!" Alina said. Alina helped me up as Cynthia pushed past me and her dark brunette hair whipped me in the face slightly. I think she got her "cut eye" look perfect by practicing on me, I joked with Alina. The inside of the cabin looked like a typical outdoor cabin. Rustic and it had this musty smell to it. It was big, with 4 bedrooms, one bathroom, a small kitchen, and dining space. It also had a cozy little fireplace with a sitting area. All of a sudden, there was this crash near the back of the cabin.

"What was that?!" Alina exclaimed, moving to stand behind me.

"I don't know; let's go find out…" I said. So, all three of us grabbed a pan and started to walk towards the back of the cabin, following the noise.

"BOO!" the boys yelled, jumping out from the shadows. We started swinging out pans before we realized it was just the boys. Thankfully, they managed to dodge the pans just before they could hit them, and they laughed.

"I never knew Nancy Drew used frying pans to attack suspects," Dustin laughed.

"What is wrong with you guys?!" I yelled, looking straight at James, who was pushing his dirty blond hair back in its place. He just shrugged, not looking sorry at all.

"Stupid boys!" Alina exclaimed. After a long pause, we all burst into laughter and walked back to the kitchen.

We searched through the cabinets until we found some potatoes and fruits, and in the freezer was some chicken and peas. We took it all and made dinner, collectively agreeing we would write a note to explain and tell them we would buy them more. "Hey, boys, do you want to go see if you could find some firewood? It's getting a bit chilly in here," I said as I shivered. "I guess so…" Dustin sighed, jokingly pretending he didn't want to. James gave me a quick kiss before the two of them went out.

"Looks like you and James are doing well…" Cynthia said as if she knew something I didn't. "Well, yeah, why wouldn't we? We are engaged…" I replied, confused.

"Whatever you say," she shrugged.

Alina, feeling the tension, asked, "So, have you guys set a date yet?"

"We have! December 31st, 2019." I stated proudly. "So soon?" both girls asked.

"Yeah, we want a small wedding and figured, why should we wait when we could start a whole new decade together as husband and wife," I smiled happily.

"Plus, she wants to be a winter bride," James said as he dusted the snow off his boots, dropping the logs on the floor. Cynthia muttered something but just loud enough for only me to hear. "People that rush into weddings means they are probably having trouble." I just ignored her statement and continued to cook.

After we had all eaten, we snuggled up in front of the fire.

"Wish we had marshmallows," Alina said.

"Yeah…oh! I know! We could play truth or dare?" Dustin suggested.

"What are we 13?" Cynthia said snobbishly. "Well, we might as well make the best out of a bad situation," James said chirpily, "but before we do that, I'm going to go get some more wood for the fire," he said.

"I'll help," Cynthia said with a smile, looking at me. The two of them put on all their winter gear and headed outside.

Dustin and I began to clear up. "How are you doing?" he asked

"I'm fine, just tired," I replied shortly.

"No, I mean, how are you doing?" he repeated, this time elongating each word. The way he asked the question reassured me that I could vent to him, so I told him about the doubts I had because of the wedding, work stress, and overall life stress. He just smiled and said, "Well, once we get back, I'll be more than happy to help."

"Thank you," I told him sincerely.

I then realized that James and Cynthia were taking a bit long, so I went to see if I could spot them through one of the windows. I managed to see them through a small window in one of the bedrooms. What I couldn't figure out was what they were saying. It seemed as if they were arguing about something, but I couldn't quite figure it out. I noticed a sudden turn of their heads, prompting me to duck and retreat back into the kitchen. They returned quietly not long after, and we all resumed our seats by the fireplace. About an hour later, James and I exchanged goodnights and retired to the room we had claimed. Yet, something inside urged me to ask what had transpired. "What were you and Cynthia talking about?" I asked him. "Nothing," he started, looking over at me, "just some small talk about the wedding and life," he finished.

"Well, it didn't look like nothing to me," I said in a snarky tone, removing the pillows from the bed and tossing them to the side. "Oh, don't start with me, Bailey," he snapped. We could faintly hear Dustin say to the girls: "looks like they're fighting again."

"See, even our friends know when we fight, and I am tired of it. So just stop it," he said, gesturing to where our friends were through the wall.

"I am just stating facts. When it comes to the two of you, it always looks more than what it should be," I said.

"Enough Bailey! That's it. I am not doing this again. You are the one that I am marrying. I can't keep going through this same argument." He said angrily as he got under the covers. I crawled in, joining him.

"I love you. No one else," he whispered as he moved in to kiss me. I just turned to my side to stare at the wall as I heard him sigh goodnight as he moved into another position.

The next morning, I woke up to the clanking of pots and pans in the kitchen, but no James beside me.

I threw on some clothes and left the room to see Dustin and Alina cooking breakfast. I heard the water running in the bathroom and asked who was there.

"Cynthia," Alina replied without turning around. "That's odd, where's James then?" I wondered.

"You mean he wasn't in bed with you?" Dustin asked.

"No, when I woke up, he was gone. I assumed he was out here."

"We haven't seen him or heard him all morning," said Dustin. Sensing that something was off, I put on my boots and coat and stepped outside to see if he might have gone for a walk. The air was still cold, and the snow had accumulated to a depth that was difficult for my 5-foot frame to manage. The minute I stepped into the snow, I sank, but I pulled through like a sledge dog being told to mush. Off in the distance, I saw what looked like a figure lying in the snow.

My heart began to race as I pushed forward towards the body, not caring that I was getting wet. The closer I got, the brighter the red on the snow was. When I finally reached it, I could not make out the body, but I hoped it wasn't who I thought it was. I bent down and rolled the body over. And my worst nightmare came true. There, lying lifeless and frozen in the snow, was James. I screamed and lifted his head to rest it on my lap. It looked like he was bludgeoned to death. The blood was frozen. I just held him and cried. I didn't think anyone had heard the scream, but the three of them did and came rushing out, and with each look, I heard their gasps and cries. Dustin knelt down to hold me, trying to pry me away from James' body as I grieved.

"We should head back to the cabin and call the police." He said, pulling me to my feet and catching me when I stumbled.

"Wait, guys! Look!" Alina exclaimed, pointing to James' jacket. There, on his jacket, was a paper pinned that read "GUILTY" in big, bold letters. No one could recognize the writing. We all helped lift his body and carried it back to the cabin, placing him in a comforter and wrapping him up. The four of us just sat there trying to figure out what to do, trying to get over our shock. Like last night, there was no cell service, and due to extreme weather alerts, it didn't seem like anyone was coming to our rescue anytime soon. The cacophony of silence was starting to drive me crazy. I sat there, thinking about all the different scenarios. I abruptly got up and walked towards the room we had placed James's body in. I reached out my hand to turn the knob....

'Knock! Knock! Knock!' I was woken up by the sound of someone knocking on the room door. I shot up from the bed. "Who is it?" I asked suspiciously.

"It's Helen…"

"Helen?" I whispered as I ran to the door to let her in. "What are you doing here? How did you know where I was?"

"That police officer Sam, I think his name was. He came to the hospital asking me all sorts of questions about you. I told him what I could. I got worried about you, so I asked him where I could find you. He gave me his address," She explained.

"Well, it is good to see you, Helen."

"Glad to hear it. I hope you're hungry. I bought some Chinese food and a guest. "She said, handing me a take-out bag.

"A… a guest?" I asked, confused, trying to look behind her. "Yeah, he'll be here in a bit," she said as she walked in.

"He?" I whispered to myself. Just as I sat down, there was another knock at the door. I got up to answer it. I reached for the door handle slowly. A part of me was hoping it would be Ethan. I opened the door and standing in front of me was a tall handsome man, who kind of looked like Chris Evans. He had a muscular build, brown hair that was combed back yet fluffy, a beard that attached perfectly to the lineup, and green eyes. He gave me a sweet and charming gentlemanly smile and held out his hand. "Aiden. Aiden Newman."

I reached out and shook his hand and said, "Bailey Clarke." The handshake lingered longer than I expected, but no one pulled away until Helen said: "Aiden, is that you?" "Yes, it is Aunt Helen," he said as he brushed past me to go hug her. I closed the door and walked back to the bed. He joined me on the bed, General Tao's chicken takeout in hand. "Bailey, darling, this is my nephew. He's a lawyer, and I asked him to represent you," she said excitedly.

"Sorry, a lawyer?" I asked.

"Yeah, you know, the kind that works in the courtroom," he said.

"Yeah, I know the kind," I giggled. "But how did you know I would need a lawyer?"

Helen, who I had completely forgotten was still in the room, jumped in, saying, "Well, when that officer came by the hospital, he made it seem as if this case could be a little more serious. This led me to believe that the blood on your clothes could only be that of an accident. So, as soon as he left, I called up my nephew," she said with a smile.

"Thank you. I do appreciate it, but I have no money to afford a fancy lawyer", I said as I got up to get a glass of water. Aiden walked over, smiled and said, "Don't worry about money. I'm going to take your case on pro-bono. As a favour to my aunt and you." I just looked at him and smiled.

We went to join Helen at the table and started to eat.

Chapter 5

"Well, I am full. I think I am going to turn in early," said an exhausted Helen. Aiden and I cleaned up as Helen began to snore. After we were down, Aiden asked me if I wanted to go for a walk, and I agreed. After all, how could I say no to someone helping me for free? So, we went out, closing the door behind us ever so quietly.

The two of us walked in silence for a bit before we both said, "So tell me…" we laughed, and he told me to go first.

"So, Mr. Big Shot Lawyer, tell me about you?"

"Well…I was born here in Innisfree. My parents died in a car accident by a drunk driver in my first year of Law school. However, the guy only got 400 hours of community service, and his license was suspended for a year."

"Oh, I'm so sorry," I said.

"It definitely motivated me to complete my degree and put guys like that behind bars," he said, "after that, I went to live with my aunt Helen, and the rest is history. How about you, Ms. Clarke?"

"Well, I grew up as an only child. Parents live back in Midland. I am a student at Redlands University. I've been here for about two years now and still not the biggest fan of the isolated countryside. After that, well, I don't exactly remember. I lost some memories of the night of the accident."

"So why are you a person of interest?" he asked, giving me a confused look.

"I don't know. They arrested me earlier today, showed me some pictures of my fiancé and friends murdered, and tried to accuse me."

"What?!" he exclaimed. "Did you say anything to them that could disprove your innocence?" he asked urgently.

"No. All I told them is that I don't remember and that I woke up in a hospital bed."

"Good! We can work with this." I smiled at him, and he continued, saying, "Let's continue this tomorrow morning," and we walked back to the motel.

The next morning, Aiden woke me up with some coffee and doughnuts.

"½ fat cream and two sugars." He said, handing me a cup and a bag.

"I like full-fat cream" I smiled at him. He just shook his head with a smile and sat across from me.

"mmm…Where's Helen?" I asked while stuffing the doughnut into my mouth.

"She left for work. But it gives us a whole day to get your case straightened out. Then we'll head to the police station get a statement, and proceed with necessary actions when need be. How does that sound?"

"Sounds like a plan," I replied. After breakfast, we sat down and started working on my case. He had laid out all his lawyer tools to a T. Everything was straight and concise. "Okay, so let's get started," he said, placing the tape recorder right in the middle of the table.

"So, Mrs. Clarke…" he started.

"Bailey. Please call me Bailey," I interrupted. He looked up from his notepad briefly and smiled at me as he continued on.

"Alright, Bailey…can you walk me through everything you remember? The more details in chronological order you can give me, the easier it will be."

I took a deep breath and began. "The first thing I can remember was waking up in the hospital with a pounding headache. Your aunt, I... I mean Helen, the head nurse there. She told to me that I had suffered from a pretty intense fall that had put me in a coma for three days.”

“How did you get to the hospital?” he questioned.

“She told me that a man by the name of Ethan had found me and brought me in.”

“Ethan?” Aiden glanced up, just enough for me to catch the confusion in his eyes as I unraveled another piece of my life story. He lifted his head fully, clasped his hands together, and continued on, “So this Ethan…what is his last name? Have you seen him since, or do you know where he is?”

“I, uh, I only saw him the one time at the hospital when he introduced himself. Then he told me to meet him at the cabin.” “And did you?” he inquired.

“Well, yes, we talked, but he wouldn’t tell me anything. The next morning, he was gone, and I never heard from him again.”

“Hmm… okay,” he said, writing something down, “So Bailey, can you try walking me through what happened at the sugar bush factory?”

“I don’t remember. Everything comes back to me in pieces.” I told him.

“Okay, what can you remember? We’ll work on the rest later.” “The last thing I dreamt of was finding my fiancé’s dead body lying in the snow.”

“So, you found the body?” he asked, looking up once more.

“Yes. I had woken up, and James wasn’t in the bed or outside in the kitchen with everyone. I figured maybe he went for a walk. When I went outside in the distance, I saw his body lying in the snow. On his coat was a pinned sign that said ‘Guilty.’”

He asked me to continue, but I could feel myself choking up as I continued. “We brought the body…”

“We?” he interrupted.

"Yeah, there were five of us on this trip. Dustin, Cynthia, and Alina. We wrapped him in a carpet and put him in the room." I explained.

"Okay, what happened next?"

"Well, I was woken up by Helen, so I don't know."

"What about the others? Would they know?" he asked, moving forward to me.

"No…all of them except Dustin and I are dead, and Dustin is still unconscious.

"How can you explain that you're the only one to have survived," he asked. He sat in silence for a minute. Then he turned off the tape recorder, looked me straight in the eyes, and asked the question everyone would soon be asking: "Did you kill them?"

I just stared back, eyes blown wide, the shock evident on my face, and with confidence, I exclaimed: "NO!"

His voice began to rise higher and more heatedly, and he said: "But you don't remember? Is there a possibility that you killed your loved ones?"

I pushed myself up onto my elbows, leaned forward to meet his face in the middle of the table, and yelled right back at him.

"Not even the slimmest of chances. I am not a killer, and I know deep down in my heart of hearts I could never kill!" I fiercely yelled.

Aiden just sat back in his chair, seemingly unaffected by my outburst, and said, "Good. You are ready for the courts." He stretched and said: "Let's take a break. I could use some pizza; how about you?"

"Yeah, I could eat," I said, my anger gone away. We both got up to grab our coats and leave. We pulled up to a small pizzeria. 'Carlos' Pizzeria: Where every pizza is made with love.

"Interesting," I said as I got out of the car.

"It's the best pizza joint. Come on, you'll like it," Aiden said enthusiastically, practically pushing me into the place. It was quite crowded when we walked in. I followed him through the mazes of tables and chairs to this tiny booth. The waiter came over and said, "Eh! Aiden! Long time no see. Who's the pretty lady?"

"Hey, Carlos. This is Bailey; she's new here." Aiden said. Carlos turned to me and said, "Aren't you the girl being accused of murdering those kids up at the sugar bush?"

I was flabbergasted and didn't know just quite how to respond. Thankfully, Aiden butted in. "Allegedly, but with my help, she will be cleared of all charges because she didn't do it," he said, shooting a look at Carlos.

"Well, in that case, you are in great hands." Carlos said to me, then turned to Aiden and said, "I'll be back with your regular," then jetted off to the kitchen. Aiden could see I was tense.

"Just relax," he said, cupping my hands in his.

After we had ordered some drinks and waited for our food, Aiden excused himself to go to the bathroom. When he got up, I saw a pretty groovy looking jukebox with lights, which played funky oldies from the 70's and 80's. I looked out the window, realizing Aiden was right — I needed to calm down. It felt good to finally escape my own thoughts and just enjoy the moment. The sun was shining, and the day seemed perfect. But that feeling didn't last long. In the glass, I caught the reflection of a tall man approaching our table, each step bringing him closer. "Bailey?" he said with a deep voice and demanding tone. I knew just who it was. I turned to him, a smile on my face, and said: "Officer Sam, how nice to see you."

"Nice to see you are still in town," he grinned.

"What are you keeping track of me or something?" I asked. "No, not at all. Bad joke, but it doesn't hurt me to see you," he said. I just looked at him intensely, "come on, not even a smile?" he asked.

"You accused me of murdering my friends, and I am supposed to be nice?"

Just then, Aiden walked out of the bathroom, and seeing Sam at our table made him rush back to me.

"Don't you know questioning a person without their lawyer is a breach, Sam?" Aiden said, standing behind him. Sam just lifted his head and turned around.

"So, you are representing her. I should have guessed," replied Sam, shaking his head lightly.

"What game are you playing this time, Sam? Is this some new detective angle? Question people in public spaces?"

"Calm your big shot jets down, Aiden. I was here getting lunch and ran into Bailey. We didn't even talk about the case." Aiden glanced over at me, and I gave him a nod in agreement to confirm what Sam had said. The two of them had this stare down, which made me uncomfortable and prompted me to jump in and say, "I was just thanking Sam for putting me up in the Bed and Breakfast."

"What a gentleman" Aiden said in a sarcastic tone, not breaking his eye contact with him. "Something you can learn, Aiden. Anyway, I have to get back to work," Sam stated, turning to me, "have a good rest of your day, and no more hospital visits, okay?" he said with a smile and wink, and then he left.

Aiden reclaimed his seat across from me. "So, Sam put you up in the motel?"

"Yeah, it was quite nice of him." Aiden just shook his head. "Please do not trust him. He's just out for his career." I could sense that he was about to ask about the hospital remark, so I quickly changed the subject.

"Seems like you two are the best of friends," I said sarcastically.

"He and I went to high school together. He was always better at everything. Finally, I proved to be better when I went to law school and won all the cases that he tried to accuse my clients of. Now he hates me, and I'm not going to lie, the feeling is mutual."

"So, I guess I can trust you to win my case?" I said with a smile.

"I will do anything to make sure you are free. This time, it's a bit more personal for me." We just shared a gaze until Carlos came back with our food.

Chapter 6

We got back to the motel late in the evening. Aiden received a call from Helen and stepped outside to take it. After about five minutes, he returned to tell me that his Aunt Helen would be staying home that night and had invited me to stay there instead of at the motel.

"Tell her I say thank you, but I would much rather stay here," I told him.

"Are you sure?" he asked.

"Yes, but you should go home and rest." "Well, I don't want to leave you alone."

"I am sure I will be fine. Don't worry." I insisted, shoving him lightly towards the door. He smiled, hugged me, and then left. Once the door closed behind him, I turned on the water, let it heat up, and filled the tub. I could feel the steam flowing through the air, fogging up the glass mirror. I stepped into the tub and sat down, the warm water hugging my body like a blanket. The feeling was amazing. I could feel the tension and stress just melt away. I closed my eyes and just sank into the warmth.

"Where are you going?" Dustin asked.

"I have to see him; I have to see him one last time." I could hear Dustin run towards me. He grabbed me and tried to pull me back; I struggled to get out of his grip.

"You can't do that to yourself. Listen to me!" he yelled, turning me around so that we were face to face, "you can't. He wouldn't want you to see him like that." I knew he was right. I just fell into his arms, letting the tears flow. We sat down with the other girls.

"What the hell was that?" Cynthia asked.

"He's dead!" Alina said, still in shock at the situation. "Someone bashed his head. He was murdered! He was murdered in his own blood!" I said, raising my head up slowly.

"We can't keep talking about this. We need a plan." Dustin, being the voice of reason, said, calming us all down before rationally thinking about the situation. "Who was the last one to see James?" he asked.

"Bailey, obviously," Cynthia said while trying to insinuate.

"Yes, because I would kill my fiancé." I snapped back, glaring at her.

"No one is blaming anyone," Dustin said. He turned to me and continued on "Did James ever leave in the middle of the night or anything?"

"No. I just woke up, and he wasn't there," I said, choking back more tears.

"Why would someone write guilty and sick it to him?" it was a question to which no one had an answer.

"Do you think someone is out here?" Alina asked, shaking. "Oh, grow up, Alina," Cynthia snarled, "There is no one here. You've been watching too many horror movies." "Well, then why did someone write guilty?" Alina screamed back, looking at each of us.

"Okay, okay. There is no sense in arguing again. The best thing we can do is stay calm. Lock the doors and come up with a plan."

"Why don't we go check the car? Maybe we could use it to get close enough to a town and call for help?" I suggest.

"That's a good idea," Dustin replied. So, we bundled ourselves up and began the trek back to the car.

When we got there, the car was almost completely covered in snow. We brushed it off and got inside. Dustin put the key in the ignition and turned. All we got was some sputtering noise. We exchanged a look and then moved to pop the hood. Staring down into the dark mess of the engine, we froze—someone had cut the wires. Maybe Alina was right. Maybe we weren't alone in the woods after all.

As we walked back to the cabin, we debated whether or not to tell the girls. "It would just scare them even more," he said.

"But they have a right to know what we know. Unless you think telling people the truth is beneath you?"

Dustin just stopped dead in his tracks, turned to me, and said, "Don't know where the hostility is coming from. But I just think it is better not to freak out or cause unnecessary stress. For any of us. However, if you want to tell them, we can." The rest of our walk was filled with silence and thinking. When we reached the steps, Dustin stopped and looked away. I could see he was waiting for me to decide, but I just brushed past him and walked inside. The girls were waiting at the kitchen table, bags packed. "I'm sorry. It looks like we can't leave right now," I said, dusting my boots off and removing my scarf.

"Why not?!" they both exclaimed. Dustin jumped in, saying, "Someone cut the wires on the car."

"I knew it. We aren't alone! Someone is out here tormenting us." Alina yelled out.

"The questions are who? And why?" Dustin said, looking around the room.

"New rule: we do everything in twos, and we keep the doors locked at all times," I said sternly. They all agreed.

That evening, we all cooked dinner together and tried to forget what happened. But I knew all of us were eyeing the door that hid the first dead body.

"I can't take this anymore," Alina said, standing up. "I need to go for a walk."

"I'll join you," said Dustin, and the two of them headed outside. This just left Cynthia and me alone. For once, she was a bit more pleasant.

"I think I'm going to go for a shower," she said, standing up as well. I just nodded. Before heading for her shower, she came over to me; I shuffled backwards a bit. She pulled me close and hugged me, whispering, "I am so sorry. For everything." Then she left, leaving the door ajar.

I stood and went to wash the dishes, trying to figure out exactly what she meant by that. After a while, I decided I could use some fresh, cool winter air as well, so I stepped onto the porch, and I was still close by if anything happened. After about fifteen minutes or so, I saw Alina and Dustin walking back, and I took a breath of relief. They approached the stairs before Alina said, "Bailey, what are you doing out here? You're supposed to be with Cynthia."

"She went for a shower; it is not like anything crazy will happen. Besides, I can hear her if something was to." We walked back inside.

"Cynthia! Dustin and Alina are back!" I shouted. "Cynthia, come on out, or else you'll turn into a prune."

Alina laughed.

"Cynthia, come on," Dustin yelled in a joking way as he brushed the snow off his hair. However, when we never received an answer, we got concerned.

"I'll go check on her," Alina said. Dustin and I were just about to make ourselves comfortable on the couch when we heard Alina scream. We jumped up and ran over to the bathroom. To our horror, the bath was filled with bloody water, and right in the middle of it was Cynthia, her throat slit.

I jolted awake as my head slipped underwater; my eyes sprung open. I felt as if someone was pushing me down.

The water had turned red. I jolted upright, relieved to realize it was only a vision. Grabbing my towel, I watched as the water swirled down the drain. I felt a wave of numbness come over me, which convinced me that maybe I could use a cup of coffee and cake. I got changed into some decent-looking pajamas and went downstairs to the 24-hour diner.

"Bailey," a cheerful voice said as the door chimed. It was Mary-Ellen. I walked over to the diner counter and pulled up a seat. Mary-Ellen came over.

"What brings you here?" she asked.

"I thought I could use a coffee fix and maybe some dessert?" I smiled.

"I know exactly what you need. I'll be back in a jiffy," she said, pouring coffee into a mug before turning to walk away.

"Twice in one day," said a familiar voice a little way down the counter. I looked to my left and sat three stools down from me was Officer Sam. I just rolled my eyes before saying, "I'm not in the mood, officer."

"Sam. How many times do I have to tell you? Call me Sam." He walked over holding a devil's food cake. "I come bearing gifts," he said. I took the cake as he sat down beside me. "So, where's your little guard dog?"

I just looked at him, "Okay, I'm sorry," he said apologetically. "Look, let's just keep case talk off-limits tonight, okay?" he asked. I just continued stuffing my face with cake, not even looking up once. "Deal?" he repeated. "Mhmm…" I replied.

After two cake slices and four cups of coffee, Mary-Ellen came over. "Looks like you enjoyed it," she states with a smile, collecting our dishes.

"Yeah, it was all really good, but I should head back up and get some sleep," I said, stifling a yawn.

"I'll walk you up," Sam said, standing up. "No, you don't have to; I'll be fine."

"Please, I want to," he pleaded. "Alright," I agreed.

"I'll be back in a bit, El, and then we'll head home," he said to Mary Ellen before leaving.

The walk back to my room was completely silent. When we got to my door, I said: "Well, this is me." I opened the door to go in, but before I could, Sam stopped me.

"Look, I'm going to be honest with you," he started, "tomorrow is the first court hearing trial, and Aiden will do anything he has to win."

"Isn't that what I want?" I asked.

"Yeah, but just be careful of him. Please."

"Funny, he told me the same thing about you. Except he's a top lawyer, and you are trying to convict me of murder."

"No, that's…"

"Goodnight, Sam," I said, closing the door behind me.

I got all ready for bed, curled under the covers, hoping to finish the vision. I closed my eyes, thinking about the last thing I saw, before falling asleep.

On the mirror behind us, written in the water condensation, was the word 'GUILTY. I couldn't contain it; I ran to the sink and threw up.

"How is this possible? You were the only one in here with her," Dustin said. I rinsed my mouth, turned to him, and asked what he meant. "Nothing, it's just odd," Dustin said, his tone mistrustful.

"Look!" Alina exclaimed, pointing outside the open window. We rushed outside to see footprints in the snow. Footprints that were significantly larger than mine appeared to have entered and exited through the same window. I snapped a picture of them, just to be safe. This meant that whoever it was, it wasn't me.

"Well, it is still your fault for leaving her alone," Dustin scolded.

"Yes, right. Sorry for not wanting to sit in the bathroom while she had a bath." We continued to argue before Alina screamed:

"STOP IT!" We both froze. "We are all being hunted. Each one of us. For something we did but have no idea what it was." She said.

We went back into the kitchen, sat down, and tried to come up with our next move.

Chapter 7

My alarm went off at 7:45 am. It was the day of the first court hearing. I put on a black dress I had bought a while ago. It was the same dress I wore when James proposed to me. I hopped into a taxi and headed to the courthouse, where Aiden was waiting for me in front of the doors. "Hey! You look great," he said once he noticed me. "Aiden, I had another vision," I said, gripping his hand in excitement, "Someone else was up there," I told him.

"So, you are saying there was a sixth person? Did you tell the police this?" he questioned.

"No. I only remembered last night after having a vision of Cynthia's death," I said, showing him the photo of the footprints.

"This is good. We will be able to use this," he said as we walked into the courtroom. He didn't seem to care that I had another vision. We took our seats, and he whispered, "Don't answer any questions unless I tell you so. Just sit here and look innocent."

"Aren't I pleading guilty?"

"Just do as I say," he said sharply. I nodded, a bit scared of him.

"All rise for Judge Samantha Carter," said the bailiff. "Good morning. Please be seated. Is everyone here?" She asked. The rest of the people chattered, "Yes, Your Honour." Then she turned to the Bailiff. He announced 'The Court versus Bailey Clarke.'

Officer Sam's lawyer or I guess you could say the town's lawyer, Kathy Simon, an elderly lady, stood up and stated the charges.

"The court charges Ms. Bailey Clarke with murder of the first degree," she stated confidently.

The judge then turned to me and asked: "Ms. Clarke, do you understand the charges being brought against you?"

I rose to my feet. "Yes, I do, and I plead…"

Aiden interjected very quickly. "Your honour, I told my client not to answer any questions as it could incriminate her."

She then turned to Aiden and asked: "Your client is taking the Fifth Amendment on whether or not she understands the charges?"

"Yes, your honour. With her recent head trauma and loss of memory, I feel like she must take the fifth on any questions or comments posed to her until we get her a complete psychiatric evaluation."

She looked me over and said, "I don't see her as a physical threat, and if you, Mr. Newman, take full responsibility for her, she can remain outside instead of in a jail cell."

"Thank you, Your Honour."

Then, we all stood as she left the room. I glanced over to see Sam smiling at me. After the court hearing, Aiden drove me back to the motel. Throughout the entire drive, I could tell he was upset with me. When we arrived, he pulled into a parking spot and we just sat there.

"I'm sorry; I just answered the question posed to me," I said in a soft tone.

He turned to me and said, "I told you not to say anything! You could have screwed up the case! Don't you listen?"

This side of him took me aback. He was furious. "I am sorry. I didn't know pleading not guilty to something I did not do would incriminate me."

"Well, it could have!" he snapped.

We just turned back to face the front. He gave a loud sigh and then, in a soft voice, said, "I'm sorry. I didn't mean to yell at you. I just don't want anything to happen to you. I feel a sense of protection towards you, and I just want to make all this trauma disappear."

I turned back to him and smiled. "I know," I said, "I promise from now on, I will do as you say and not speak unless you let me."

"I mean, you can still talk. Just not in the courts," he said. We both laughed.

"So, this psychiatric evaluation," I asked.

"Yeah, I think it would help your case and you as well if we can jog your memory and bring all those visions of murder to light. You know?" he said.

"I think that's a good idea."

"Well, I will set it up for you," he stated.

The next day, Aiden came to pick me up for our appointment in a rented Honda Civic. I got into the car and he politely greeted me. "Do you like the car?" he asked. "Yes, it is very nice," I replied, putting on my seatbelt. "Well, it's yours," he stated, looking at me with a smile on his face. "No. What?" I said, complexly lost for words. "I figured you would need something to help you get around if I'm not available, so here it is," he said. "I...I couldn't," I stammered. "Please take it," he said, grasping my hand in his. I put my other hand on his and said, "Alright," and we drove off. "This doctor is amazing. I have worked with him many times, and he's ready to help you remember." I hoped he could, I thought to myself. After an hour and a half of driving, we arrived at Dr. Daniel North's clinic. We waited in the room for about thirty minutes. "Sorry I'm late," he said as he stumbled into his office. "He looks like a quack," I whispered to Aiden.

"Come one, give him a chance. He's a great doctor," he replied.

"What can I do for you?" He asked as he sat in his chair behind the desk.

"This is Bailey Clarke. She is being accused of murder, but she can't tell what happened on that night. She only remembers a few moments. We are hoping you can help us with the rest of the missing puzzle pieces," Aiden said.

"What do you remember, Ms. Clarke?" the doctor inquired. "I remember finding the bodies of my friends. I remember seeing the word Guilty written on each of them. I remember footprints in the snow and running. The rest is a blur," I answered.

"Do you believe that there was a sixth person killing everyone, and he/she was hunting you guys down? And you can't remember? And therefore, you need my help to uncover the grey area?" he asked.

"Yes," I replied.

"So, you hit your head, and now you have amnesia about that night?" he asked skeptically. Before I could answer, Aiden moved forward, and with a threatening voice, he said: "I believe she is innocent. So, you either help us or don't."

I pulled him back to the chair, and the three of us stared at each other before the therapist said, "I am more than

happy to help you, but let's get one thing straight: I will not be doing this to validate your story," he said sternly.

"We stick to our jobs," Aiden agreed.

"Before we start, I want all the diagnostics from the hospital, Bailey. Then, I want you to re-undergo an MRI, neuropsychology test, an EEG test and see the difference between then and now."

"Yes, doctor," I said.

He huffed and said: "We start tomorrow at 10 am sharp."

We thanked him and left his office.

The next morning, we arrived at Dr. North's clinic. He placed me in an isolated room, and it was just me, him, and a video camera. Aiden waited outside as we started our session.

The session was full of questions about my home life and whether I was a psychopath. It lasted for about an hour.

"How was it?" Aiden asked as we walked out. "Nothing," I said.

"Well, it was our first session. Maybe a few more will help jog your memory," Aiden said hopefully. Dr. North agreed, and we set up another appointment for Friday, December 13th, at 10 am.

"Do you mind staying at my place tonight? It would help us work on the case for tomorrow's opening trial," Aiden asked.

"Yeah, sure," I said.

We stayed up for almost half the night, coming up with the best opening statements and witness lists. We tried to find every loophole the opposition could use against us. Each time Aiden sat down to write a new opening statement, it quickly followed with him crumpling up the paper and throwing it into the garbage like a basketball player.

At around 2 am, Aiden and I turned on the TV. We put on the news to hear:

'In what appears to be the most exciting yet horrific murder trial that the small town of Innisfree has seen in years, former big-shot city lawyer Aiden Newman will be delivering his opening statement tomorrow.'

This shook me up. It made me realize that this was a real-life nightmare.

"You should get some sleep. We have a big day ahead of us tomorrow," Aiden said from the desk behind me.

He walked me upstairs to the spare bedroom. "Don't worry, we will get through this together," he said as he hugged me goodnight.

Chapter 8

It was the same dress I wore when James proposed to me. I hopped into a taxi and headed to the courthouse, where Aiden was waiting for me in front of the doors. Aiden shielded me as we walked into the courtroom. We sat down, took a deep breath and waited for what felt would be one of the longest days in my life. The opposition went first.

"Those young kids had their whole future ahead of them. They were top-class students and were on the right track with life. They spent their lives practicing the catholic faith and were very family-oriented. They were a beacon of light not only to their families and friends but to everyone around them. One of them was even engaged to the defendant. But do not let that or her pathetic innocence and demeanor fool you. She had a motive for the murder. Bailey Clarke decided that she needed to play judge, jury, and executioner, and not only should her friends die, but each one should die the most gruesome and horrific death possible. The evidence will show that Bailey Clarke masterminded and savagely carried out this death plan."

Kathy sat down after delivering her opening statement. Aiden rose to give his.

"My name is Aiden Newman. The reason we are all here is to unveil the truth. The truth which the prosecution does not want you to hear. Ms. Bailey Clarke was brought into a hospital room after the accident with a head trauma and a stab wound *and* was not arrested. The reason that the police are now turning to her as a suspect is because it is convenient that she is the only survivor. The police have enormous pressure to solve this case. The prosecution does not want you to know about the sixth person who was out to kill these students. They don't want you to hear the theory of motive, and this is because they do not have one." Aiden reprised his seat as the rest of the court mumbled and chattered.

The pictures of the gruesome killings of my friends were hung up on a board for everyone to view. It made me ever so nauseous. The first witness to take the stand was the coroner.

The opposition questioned her first:

Kathy: The victims suffered a great deal of torture due to a slow death. Isn't that right, coroner?

Coroner: Yes, that is correct.

Kathy: From your analysis, how were the victims killed?

Coroner: They show no signs of struggle, which means they were taken off guard. This leads me to believe it could have been premeditated.

Kathy: Your witness counselor.

She gestured to Aiden and then the witness bench.

Aiden: Doctor, isn't it true that you cannot be sure that a sixth person could have inflicted the murders?

Coroner: It is possible, but I highly doubt it.

Aiden: Looking at the facts, Ms. Clarke is small and could not possibly carry those heavy bodies. Isn't that true?

Coroner: Yes, she is small…

Aiden: Also, James was bludgeoned to death. That takes a lot of force. The force that I'm sure my client does not have. We can test that with the carnival hammer machine.

And Cynthia's death was a throat slit, which means someone strong would have to hold her down to inflict such a clean cut. Therefore, the possibility of a sixth person, mainly being the killer is reasonable to assume.

Coroner: I guess so.

Aiden: The defendant rests.

After a day packed with statements and accusations, I returned to the motel, struggling to believe this was my life. Just then, I received a text message from Aiden. *'Dinner tonight at 7? La Bistro'.* I smiled at my phone and answered yes.

That night, I met Aiden at the restaurant. We sat, laughed, and enjoyed ourselves. It almost made us forget what had actually brought us together and what was still going on.

"I feel like everyone is looking at me?" I whispered to him.

"They are. They are looking at how amazing you look tonight", he said encouragingly. "Or maybe they think they are looking at a killer," I replied.

"Don't worry about it. Ignore them," he said.

The next morning, we went back to the doctor's office.

Aiden dropped me off in my rented car.

"I'll be back. I'm going to go do a grocery run." He said. "Sounds good to me," I said, closing the door behind me.

I went into the office for our scheduled appointment. Dr. North came in, "Let's begin where we left off," he said, "Last time you were here, we ended off with your relationship with the victims."

"We were good. James and I were ready to get married. Dustin, who was one of my closest friends, and Alina were great."

"What about Cynthia?" he asked.

"Well, we never really saw eye to eye, but it wasn't that I wanted her dead," I replied.

"So right now, you only remember how two of them died?" he asked.

"Yes," I replied.

This went on for another half an hour or so. Finally, we stood up and ended our waste-of-time session.

I went outside to see Aiden waiting for me, car running. I hopped into the car. "Hey, you? How was shopping?" I asked. "It was fine," he said abruptly.

"Someone is grumpy?" I laughed, "What's going on?"

He didn't say anything. He just started to drive fast. "Hey, Aiden, what's going on?" I asked, freaked out. He continued to ignore my questions.

He pulled into the abandoned parking lot, out of the city. He stopped the car and turned it off. He got out of the car, went to the trunk, pulled something out, and slammed it shut.

I still sat there as confused as ever. He got back into the car and tossed the bag at me. When I opened it, I found the bloody clothes I had hidden in the back. My heart started to race. "Explain this," he asked, looking out the window. I just sat there, frozen. Before I could say anything, he asked: "Do you trust me?"

"Yes! I do." I said, holding his arm.

"No! I don't think you do. I think if you did trust me, you would help me." He yelled.

"I am trying to!" I screamed back.

"Maybe this whole loss of memory is a ploy. Maybe you know it all, and you want me to look like the fool up there. Maybe you are a heartless, cold-blooded killer." He roared.

"You can't believe that?" I cried.

"I don't know what to believe anymore," he said, looking back out the window.

After a little while, he said, "Tell me you didn't do it. Tell me I am wrong, and I'll believe you, no matter the evidence."

"I didn't do it. I swear on my life." I pleaded.

"Good. Then there is no use for these clothes." He said, grabbing the bag and getting out of the car. I followed him. "What do you mean? What are you going to do?" I questioned. "It's just you and me in the big open nowhere. No one will know as long as you don't say a word," he said, lighting the clothes on fire. "Is there anything else I should know?" he asked.

"I went to the hospital to see Dustin. But he was still in a coma. That's all I swear."

"Good," he said. We just stared at the flames before he put it out. "Get back in the car, we're heading home." So, I did as he said.

Chapter 9

It was the day of the second hearing, the one where I might end up on the stand, as Aiden had mentioned if we found ourselves backed into a corner. He had prepared me for everything I needed to say during cross-examination. We went through the whole courtroom opening routine, something that should not feel so familiar and normal was. The first witness Aiden called up was Dr. North.

Aiden: Dr. North, how long have you and Ms. Clarke been working together

Dr. North: Approximately 20 hours

Aiden: And in those 20 hours, can you say that she has regained any recollection of the incident?

Dr. North: No. I performed the same tests that the hospital did and it showed that the brain swelling has come down. We have even tried hypnosis, but nothing has helped her.

Aiden: A more important question. Do you think Ms. Bailey Clarke is capable of murder? **Dr. North:** No, I do not.

After Aiden was done examining the witness, Kathy cross-examined him. After that, there was a brief recess.

Aiden said, "I'm going to put you up on the stand. Are you ready?"

"Yes!" I said confidently.

We went back to our seats. They called me up and made me swear on the Bible, to tell the truth and nothing but the truth, and then it all began.

Aiden: Ms. Bailey, could you tell us a little bit about your relationship with the victims?

Me: I was engaged to one of them and close friends with the others. We had known each other for 2 and half years now. I loved them very much.

Aiden: Why did you love them?

Me: They were my first friends when I got to university, and we did everything together. They were my second family.

Aiden: Have you ever been furiously mad with them? Mad enough that you said you would kill them jokingly, but a part of you meant it?

Me: No, of course not. Yes, they annoyed or hurt me by sometimes making plans without me, but I never wanted to see any harm come to them. I love them.

His questioning went on for a bit before he allowed Kathy to cross-examine me.

Kathy stood up and walked over to me.

Kathy: is it true, Ms. Clarke, that you were brought into the hospital with a head injury?

Me: Yes

Kathy: Is it true that when the nurse found you, your clothes were all bloody?

Me: Yes, but…

Kathy: is it also true that earlier in the week, you never hung out with James and the rest of them?

Me: Yes, but…

Kathy: So that could have given you time to plan these murders

Aiden: Objection, the counselor is insinuating

Kathy: I'll rephrase. Why did you guys take a break?

Me: I needed some time alone to process school work and all.

Kathy: It seems as if there was some blood found on your ring

Me: I found James' body and held his bare hands so… **Kathy:** And isn't it true that you hacked the hospital computer to find out where Dustin was and then ran away when confronted?

Me: Yes. I was scared, and I just wanted to see my friend.

Kathy: Then why didn't you explain that to someone? No, instead, you put on a hood and ran for your life," she said, gesturing to a screen showing surveillance footage. "Only someone guilty would do that. Don't you agree?"

I just sat there in silence.

"No further questions, your honor," she said as she reclaimed her seat beside Sam.

"You may step down now, Ms. Clarke," the judge said. I took my place beside Aiden. "You held your own very well up there," Aiden whispered.

"Well, I was trained by the best," I said, smiling. The judge set a date for the final hearing.

As we began to leave the courtroom, I could tell that Aiden was still upset with me. When he turned around to offer me a ride back to the motel, I told him he didn't have to drive me home. I preferred to walk instead. "Besides, the fresh air could be good for me," I told him, and he agreed before leaving. As I started to walk down the stairs, Sam ran past me and stopped abruptly. "Look, I am sorry about my lawyer. I told her not to go that hard on you," he said.

"Why would you do that?" I asked him.

"Because I don't think you did it anymore." He said. I was taken aback but smiled at him.

"Do you maybe want to get out of here and grab something to eat and drink?" he asked.

"I would love to," I replied. So, the two of us went back to the motel and ordered in.

We sat there laughing about some cheesy movie that was playing on channel 6. Then Sam turned to me and said: "I'm sorry for everything."

"I understand why you thought so. But no court talk tonight." I smiled.

"Deal," he said.

We continued to eat and laugh. As I was eating some pie with whipped cream, some of the whipped cream stayed on my lip. Sam took his finger and wiped it off.

We shared a long gaze and both of us started to move closer together slowly. However, before anything happened, we were interrupted by a knock on the door.

"Bailey. Open up." It was Aiden. I went to the door and opened it. "Bailey, I'm…" then he stopped. I knew he had seen Sam behind me. He pushed me aside and strutted in.

"What the hell are you doing here?" he asked Sam, the anger evident in his voice. Sam leaped to his feet, and Aiden threw the first punch. They began to fight, so I interjected, throwing myself in between the two hotheads, praying that no one would throw another punch. They stopped when they saw me.

"Aiden, it's nothing. Sam was nice enough to walk me home, and we ordered some food."

"And now I should be going," Sam said, wiping the blood off his lip.

"I think that would be best," I said. I walked him to the door.

"I'll see you again, hopefully sometime soon." He whispered.

"Yes," I replied. I closed the door behind him and looked at Aiden. He had this look on his face of pure disappointment and possible envy.

"Don't start with me," I said to him, "besides, what are you doing here?" I questioned.

"I told you not to trust him," Aiden exclaimed. "Ughh…It was just some food and drinks," I said, annoyed.

"No, it's the way he plays games to find out," he continued.

"It was innocent. We just had dinner and drinks. He said he doesn't think I carried out the murders anymore," I said, smiling.

Aiden just stared at me and said, "Can't believe you are so naive. This is the way he plays with your mind so you trust him, and then when you slip up, he'll take you down" he said. "Look, this bro, battle of the best needs to stop. And I am not involved. "I exclaimed, turning away from him to clean up the food and drinks.

Aiden just followed me and grabbed my shoulder. "You're scaring me, Aiden," I said, tensing up slightly at the touch.

"I have done everything for you, and this is how you treat me." He let his arms fall to his sides.

I put the dishes down and held his face in my hands. "I will always be indebted to you. For everything that you've done." I whispered.

I leaned in and kissed him. He kissed me back.

We stood there kissing for an undeterminable amount of time, our arms wrapped around each other. At some point, he picked me up and moved us to the bed. We sank into the movements and the peaceful sound of the night.

After everything that had happened, I couldn't sleep, tossing and turning in bed. Aiden, on the other hand, was fast asleep. The weight of being accused of murder was beginning to take a toll on my emotions. I needed to uncover the truth. I decided I had to return to the cabin. I got dressed, grabbed the keys from the nightstand, and headed to the car.

Chapter 10

The snow floated down ever so gently as I drove on the pitch-black highway. No lights other than the high beams on my car. It felt like I was driving forever. All I knew was that I needed answers to whatever my mind had locked away, hidden like a vault. Each time I pressed the brake, I felt my car sliding. James had always been the one to swap my summer tyres for winter ones.

It was about 11 pm when I reached the Sugar Bush. The road was even worse than the last time I was up here. Everything that I had remembered, like the car stalling, the five of us walking to the cabin, Ethan and I, all of it were like photo spurts in my brain.

I finally reached the cabin. I pulled up in front of it and turned off the engine. I got out of my car and scanned the premises a bit. I then grabbed my luggage from the back seat and went inside.

It was dark and cold and still had a familiar musty smell to it. I unpacked in one of the bedrooms and turned on some music.

and started dinner. I finished cooking and cleaning, then went to the bedroom. The music from the CD player trickled in, making me feel safe. Before turning off the lights, I stared at the closed bedroom across from me. I approached the room where we had laid James, stepping slowly, one foot at a time. Placing one hand flat against the door, I gripped the doorknob with the other. Then, I slowly turned the handle and opened the door. The window was open, and a gust of snow shot at me, startling me. I walked in and knelt beside the bed. Shivers ran down my spine. I didn't know if it was from the snow or knowing that a dead body had been in here, or maybe both. I became overwhelmed with it all, but I knew I had to stick to it to clear my name.

It wasn't until 2:30 am that I fell asleep in that same bed. As crazy as it sounds, I figured maybe if I slept in the same room that we had put James's and Cynthia's bodies in, it would unlock the chamber of secrets.

"WE ARE BEING HUNTED! WHAT DON'T YOU

GET!" Alina wailed.

"We just need to calm down and think rationally", I started to say before being interrupted.

"Rationally? RATIONALLY?! There is no rational thinking at this point. Alina is right; we're being hunted one at a time for something we don't even know, but someone else clearly does. Who's next?" Dustin yelled.

"Okay, I understand everyone is scared, but the killer only attacks when we are alone. This time, we say close. I boiled some water before stepping out for some fresh air. Maybe some tea will do us all some good." I said calmly, hoping to stop their panicking.

I got up, walked over to the counter, and started to pull three mugs down from the cabinet. Dustin walked over and started to help me.

"I didn't mean to snap at you", he began, looking apologetic, "It's just two of my best friends are dead. We could be next, and I am just freaking the hell out."

I pulled him into a hug. "I know it's scary. I'm terrified, too."

"Well, you sure have an air of calmness to you" he replied.

"I learned from the best to stay calm and to think rationally", I laughed, giving him a playful punch on his shoulder. The steam whistle noise from the kettle scared the living daylights out of us but also made us laugh just enough to forget our nerves for a bit.

Dustin handed Alina a cup, and we all sat down again. Sipping the tea and trying to come up with an escape plan. We were still going to be trapped up here because of a snowstorm and lack of cell service. We were living in every cliché horror movie invented.

"Why don't we walk to a town?" Dustin suggested. "Well, because we could die?" I said in a sarcastic voice.

"If we stay here, we could die. At least out there, we have a chance. We can stop at the car to warm up before continuing," he continued.

"Dustin is right?" Alina hesitated.

"It's our only feasible option," he said, looking at me. "Please, Bails, you know deep down I'm right, and James would want you to do anything to stay alive," he said.

He knew he would win if he used James. I would do anything for him.

"Fine! We'll go." I said with a deep breath.

We all packed up some snacks and tea and bundled ourselves up.

"Promise me when we get to a town; the first thing we do is call the police?" I said.

"I promise," Dustin replied.

We took one last look at the cabin and at the closed door that hid the bodies of our friends before setting out on the most harrowing journey of our lives.

We started to head down, which we assumed was the road or a path. We couldn't really see much since the snow covered it all like a big, white fluffy blanket. The snow began to hit us like sharp, tiny rocks against our faces as we continued to walk against it.

"It…It's…soooo.., c…c…cold" Alina chattered from the behind us.

"It w...would help if you don't think about it or t…t…talk about it", Dustin snapped.

We kept walking, and off in the white distance, we saw the black car covered with snow.

"Yessssss!" screamed Alina, picking up her pace in an awkward shuffle that could rival a penguin's.

Dustin and I looked at each other, smiles on our faces. Our walking strides became longer and more energetic. The snow and cold weren't going to keep us from getting to safety. Well, that's what we thought, at least.

I started to slow down. The other two were pretty far from me. Alina, noticing I had stopped, came running back, "Hey, Bailey, are you okay?" "I…I don't know," I said. I started to stumble, so Alina grabbed me, trying to keep me up.

"I don't feel well," I said. All of a sudden, my legs gave out, and Alina did not expect it, so she let go, and I fell. "Something's not right," I said.

"Dustin! Come back here!" Alina exclaimed. He turned around to see me fall, and he ran back over. "Bails! Bails, talk to me! What's going on?" he started to fire questions.

"I don't know. It's getting blurry," I slurred out, trying to focus on something, anything. "Okay, you have to stay with me", he prompted me. From the corner of my eye and with the little consciousness I still had; I could see Alina starting to sway. She said that she wasn't well, and then she went down. After that, I couldn't keep my eyes open, and I succumbed to the darkness.

I woke up back in the cabin. Hands and legs tied, feeling groggy from what happened. As I shook my head, hoping that would help make everything stop spinning, I saw Dustin and Alina to either side of me. They, too, were bound like cattle as well.

"Dustin! Alina! Guys! Get Up! NOW!" I started to whisper loudly. I could hear their groggy moans and groans as they regained consciousness. Alina was first to come to her senses, and her eyes went wide when she noticed where we were. Then Dustin came to. We all tried to get upright from the laid position our attacker had put us in. Once we managed to do that, we moved closer together and tried to untie each other's hands, but to no avail.

We suddenly heard heavy boots enter the cabin and pound on the carpet out in front.

"Stay quiet", Dustin instructed. The stranger was a tall man, but he wore a hood so that we could not see his face.

"I'm glad you guys are finally awake. I was beginning to think I gave you a quicker death than your comrades." The voice was muffled under the hood, but those eyes held some dark secret that the three of us knew. He poured himself a cup of tea. "Why? Why did you do it?" I asked him. He continued to stir the milk into his tea before saying: "Because they deserved it. They screwed up a bit too much. They needed to pay the price."

"What did they do that led them to be killed like animals?" I pressed. He pulled up a chair, sat down, legs crossed and said: "You have a lot of questions, for which I have all the answers, but also, your two fellow survivors here."

"What do you mean? What do they know?" I said, my voice beginning to rise.

"Why don't you ask them? Ask them what they have been hiding from you for the past 6 months," he said, gesturing to them. I looked over to them.

"Guys?" I asked.

"This man is a lunatic. He's lying. We would never lie to you," Dustin spoke up, and the killer's expression grew even colder with anger. Suddenly, he pulled a gun from his pocket. Before we could react, a shot rang out, and Dustin fell back with a cry, clutching his shoulder. Alina and I screamed, the shock settling in. The man had shot Dustin!

"Don't ever call me a lunatic. You could die right here! Right now, and you are still going to lie to her," the killer said, gesturing with the gun.

Dustin sat up, blood streaming from his shoulder and from where he had hit his head when he fell. He searched for his glasses before the killer cocked the gun and pressed it against Dustin's temple. "Come on. Tell her..." he coaxed. When no one answered, he pushed the gun even closer to Dustin's head.

"Cynthia and James have been having a secret affair." Alina yelled.

Time seemed to stop. I slowly turned to her, my heart sinking deep into my chest. "What did you just say?" I asked.

"I'm so sorry!" she exclaimed, looking at her feet, refusing to make eye contact.

"Now it's a party," said the killer.

"You both knew about this? Since when?" I said looking back at each one of them, ignoring the other man.

"Since the summer," Dustin said. I turned to glare at him. "It was when you went on your trip during that big fight you guys had. James was pretty upset. He missed you; it had already.

been a week, and you would be gone for another. I decided to take him to a bar and have a guy's night. Over there, we ran into her. We played some shot games and the next day we woke up. The two of them had confessed that they slept together, but they felt guilty about it. You came back, things weren't as they seemed and well, James found solace with Cynthia. Alina and I never condoned it," he explained.

"No, you just all decided to make me the fool and to let me marry a cheater," I snapped.

"We tried to get them to stop and tell you the truth, but we didn't know how. I am so sorry that this is how it unfolded. I really am," Dustin finished.

I just sat there. I couldn't believe it. I had no emotions. I didn't know what to feel. I was numb. The killer stepped over Dustin and knelt beside me. The killer brushed my hair back, and I tried to shuffle away from him.

"Shhhh..." he whispered. He continued to caress my face with his hand, "I know it is hard taking in all this information. Knowing that the people you loved and trusted the most were just out to play you and hurt you. Let me help you out. I will kill the rest of these slime bags. And then I'll kill you," he finished, lifting the gun back up.

I looked up at him, our eyes meeting. He could probably see my confusion as to why he wanted to kill me. "Oh, you aren't any more innocent than them, but I do actually feel bad this happened. However, I can't let you go since you've seen me and know my voice," he said.

"Please! You don't have to do this. They made a mistake. Everyone makes mistakes! You don't have to kill them," I pleaded, desperate to at least save some of my friends, even if they had lied to me.

"Yes, they do, sweetheart. They don't care about anyone but themselves. They use you for your good nature, but when they don't need you, they toss you out," he said. He got up and started walking around tormenting the other two with the gun. He turned back to me, "But here is what I'll do. You, my little princess, get to decide by which method they will die." He placed the gun on the table and then pulled out a hunting knife and laid it beside the gun.

I started to fiddle with the tape against a screw sticking out from the sofa. The killer walked closer to me, and I lunged. He pushed me, and I fell back, banging my head on the corner of the kitchen table before hitting the ground. Then he grabbed the knife and placed the cold stainless-steel hunting knife against my neck.

"I was going to give you a choice, but I guess now I'll just make the decision for us."

"Please let her go", Alina cried out.

"SHUT UP!" the killer yelled back, pointing the knife at her for a second before turning back to me. He traced the flat side.

of the knife from my neck to my belly button as he whispered, "This is going to hurt," and he pushed the knife halfway into my stomach, causing me to scream. I heard the other two yell my name.

"I wish it hadn't come to this. I really wanted to go easy on you, but you just made it worse for yourself and them," he said angrily as he drove the knife in further. He took it out in one swift movement and tied me to the kitchen chair, giving me a front-row seat to my friend's slaughters. The stab wound was bleeding profusely, and I was starting to feel hazy from the blood loss. All I could hear was screaming, and the world slowly blurred. I could hear their pleading, but I was helpless. I couldn't do anything to stop this. Slowly, I lost my grip on consciousness and slipped into the darkness.

When I woke up, I noticed that a towel had been wrapped around my stab wound. A few feet away from me, I saw both of my friends lying in a pool of their blood. I felt sick, and silent tears began to stream down my face. I felt the tape that held my hand being cut. Anxiety ran through my veins the way blood does, but this time, I was very aware of my heart pounding in my chest. The killer lifted me by the arm.

"This is what you did. This is on you," he yelled, "now you're going to help me clean up this mess. Get up! Pick her arms up", he ordered. I stood up with a wince, still in excruciating pain, and grabbed Alina's arms, helping the killer lift her body.

The snow crunched as the killer, and I brought the bodies into the forest. We finally returned to the cabin. I was holding the sharp knife covered in blood. It slipped out of my hand and clattered against the cabin steps, sounding like a china plate being smashed.

The nervousness and anxious feeling began to take over. Had someone seen or heard the noises? Were the cops on their way up? We walked back into the cabin.

"If only the walls had ears," he said. The cold shuddered down my spine as I cleaned the bloody mess in the Cabin. He hid the knife in the loose floorboards.

My eyes shot open. I ran into the kitchen to find that loose board. My vision served me correctly; there it was, as clear as day. The knife, which had killed three of my friends, was sitting behind this wooden board.

"Well, well, well, what do we have here," a voice behind me said. I quickly spun around to see Officer Sam standing right behind me. His arms were crossed and he had that same unpleasant look on his face. I knew he wasn't messing around. I looked up at him and said: "I know who killed them, Sam."

Sam pulled me to my feet and then pushed me to the sofa.

"Sam, I know what it looks like, but I know who killed them," I exclaimed.

"Shut up! I thought you would be more careful. Maybe I was wrong. Maybe you are the murderer," he said.

"You don't really believe that, do you?" I asked.

"I don't know what to believe anymore," Sam said as he sat beside me on the couch.

"What's wrong?" I asked, moving closer to him.

"There is no easy way to say this to you, but Dustin was found dead."

"Dead?!" "DEAD?!" I started crying, "I didn't do it if that's what you are thinking," I said in between sniffles and tears.

"I know you didn't. But someone did, and it is possible that it was Aiden" I shot him a look. "Look at it this way; he came to the motel very weirdly and at an odd time. Besides, five minutes after I left, I got a call that there was an emergency at the hospital." I couldn't wrap my head around that Aiden; my Aiden could be a killer.

"How did he die?" I asked softly.

"From the looks of it, he was suffocated by a pillow," he said. Sam wrapped me in his arms. "Now, I need you to be honest with me and I need you to understand that I am the only one that can get you out of this now.”

I started to explain all of my visions of murder, and slowly, piece by piece, we made a whole new foolproof plan to prove my innocence. There was no way I was going down for murder.

“Looks like we’re all we got. So, let’s come clean with everything; I’m not going to let you go to jail. I love you, Bailey,” Sam said.

Chapter 11

I heard a car pull up to the cabin. It was him. Ethan. Finally, after what felt like an eternity, he was back. The man with whom I had an affair while engaged to James. The man who had promised me that everything would be okay. But where had he been when I needed him? It was time to find out.

I stood in the middle of the cabin in the same red dress I wore the very first time we'd met. He opened the door and kicked it shut behind him. He briskly walked towards me and kissed me with passion.

"I'm glad you're safe and this is all over", he said. I gave him half a smile. "You have no idea how worried I was about you every single day. But it just wasn't safe for us to be seen together."

"I understand," I said.

"But…but now we can be together just like we wanted. Just like you said when you came up with the plan to kill them all," he said, "my bags are packed, full tank of gas. Let's go!" he exclaimed as he grabbed my hand, pulling me towards the door. I stopped him with a kiss.

"We still have some time," I said.

"Oh, really?" he replied, trying to lead me to the bed.

"Mhmm…so I think I'm going to go for a shower first," and with that, I walked to the bathroom, closed the door and turned on the water.

After a little while, I heard the wailing of sirens off in the distance, and I was sure Ethan heard them as well because, within seconds, he busted down the bathroom door and lunged at me. He wrapped his hands around my neck. Holding me against the wall and asking me, "What did you do? How did they know we were here?"

"Ethan", I tried to say with what was still within me. I could feel his grip getting tighter and the sirens getting louder, but I couldn't wait until they came because I wasn't sure I would be alive. I reached for my cosmetic kit and pulled out the knife I had hidden in it. Ethan's eyes were locked on me, and I could see a killer within him.

I grabbed the knife, and with every ounce of strength I had, I stabbed him with the cold, sharp knife and pulled it back out. He stumbled away from me, causing me to drop to the floor, desperately trying to regain my breath. Holding his side and staring deep into my eyes, he said: "H-How…How could you do this?" Finally, four 4 squad cars pulled up to the cabin. I balled myself up in the corner of the room and let the tears and terror take over.

Sam was the first to enter the cabin after confirming there was no immediate danger outside. He headed straight for the bathroom, only to be met with the bloody scene inside. . He checked Ethan's pulse, which was still there, then ran over to me. He picked me up and took me outside. The paramedics wrapped me in a warm towel, and Sam said, "The worst of it is over. We have him, and no one will hurt you now." I gave him a small, grateful smile. He proceeded to talk, but I just drowned him out when Ethan came out on a gurney, handcuffed. He was somewhat conscious, and we had a brief moment of eye contact before he was lifted into an ambulance, and the doors were shut.

The next few weeks were full of courtroom visits and testimonies. Until December 30th, when I turned on the television, far away from all the drama to hear:

"ETHAN WOODS HAS OFFICIALLY BEEN FOUND GUILTY OF FIRST-DEGREE MURDER OF THE FOUR VICTIMS: JAMES DONOVAN, CYNTHIA SHADE, ALINA CARLTON, DUSTIN MURRAY & THE ATTEMPTED MURDER OF BAILEY CLARKE."

You are probably at the end of the letter now. Furious with me, and you probably want to kill me. Before you start making any wild plans, let me finish. You asked me that night at the cabin how I could do something like this, but the real question you should have asked is why. Well, here is why: YOU! You promised me you would always have my back, and just like James and the rest of them, you lied. You left. You found someone else while I gave you everything and was being charged with murder. What was her name again? Ahh yes,

Courtney. Did you promise her the world? Did you kill for her? Nooo…you just wanted some much-needed attention since I couldn't give it to you.

It was genius of you to cut the car wires after we left. The set-up was perfect. I knew the minute I planned it all, it would be flawless, and I was right. The shocking thing was just lucky a coincidence. The problem was you weren't supposed to kill the other two. The useless ones, but maybe it was for the best. When I killed James and Cynthia, it was something I never felt before. Mind you, I did feel a bit bad afterwards, for a bit, but man, oh man. James' death was easier, sort of. You only helped me clean up the mess, but you weren't there when it all went down. After I heard Cynthia and him arguing, I knew it had to be about the affair they were having. As you know, it was going on for a while.

That night, I couldn't take it. James had to go first. As we got ready for bed, I glanced over at the lamp on the nightstand beside my side of the bed. It was the perfect murder weapon. Halfway through the night, I confirmed everyone was asleep. I could see James was sleeping on his stomach. I picked up the white lamp, and in the dark, I struck the back of his head. The lamp became bloodier and bloodier with every blow. The blood flicked off him and spattered on the bed sheets, pillow and me. Every bash got stronger as I cried, knowing that he deserved it all. Every lie he told me, every kiss and touch was fake! And this was the consequence. You helped me in dragging the body outside and cleaning up the mess. I couldn't lift such a heavy body on my own.

Next was Cynthia. With her murder, I had to be very careful. The other two were already spooked and on high alert. When she said she was going to go shower, I told the other two the go for a walk and quickly grabbed the sharpest knife from the kitchen drawer. She soaked in the tub, eyes closed. The timing could not be better. The feeling was so strong. I started at her thinking about her and how it must have been when she was with James. Every bitchy comment, every cut eye she ever gave me, made the blood in my body boil. So, without a second guess, I knelt down and killed her. The initial spatter of blood illuminated the stainless-steel blade like a hologram in the break of day. The weight of the penetration on the blade intensified; metal met flesh like a hot knife slicing into butter. Spurts of blood turned into a surging fountain as her jugular was severed. The blood seeped into the bathwater, turning it into the River Nile from the ten plagues of Egypt.

The other two screaming bloody murder as you threatened them into confessing their knowledge about the affair. Your idea to stab me was brilliant. Even all the other stuff, like the footprints and hiding the murder weapons, made them trust that I did nothing. However, the other two were never supposed to die. When I regained consciousness, there they were, lying dead on the floor. At least, that is what I thought.

As we pulled their bodies into the forest, you had this look of satisfaction in your eyes. It horrified me. When I started to doubt it all, you pulled me back into reality. "If only the walls had ears," you said.

The cold shuddered down my spine as I cleaned the mess in the Cabin. Why couldn't it be simple? All I ever asked was for the truth. The dark side about which I warned everyone about had prevailed. It wasn't like I wanted this, but they needed to be taught a lesson. They took me to be the fool for far too long. And so did you.

You had underestimated just who you were dealing with. How many times did I have to prove myself? To you? To James? To everybody? Finally, I made it an air-sealed tight case with all the evidence pointing to you; even if you had gone to the deepest parts of the Earth, it would always point to you. So, it was sine qua non that you accepted your faith.

The next question you probably have is: How did I manage to pull this off? Well, at first, it was easy because I didn't remember anything. As time went on, all the visions of the murders came back to me. It wasn't until after the last vision a few nights ago that I went back to the sugar-bush cabin and found the only thing that could tie me to the murders. The murder weapon, the knife that I had stabbed you with. The minute I picked it up, it all came rushing back to me like a tidal wave.

You see, my friends hurt me so badly that we both knew a quick death just wouldn't do. James sleeping with Cynthia. My enemy, his ex-girlfriend. That was the motive. The other two were just collateral for knowing that those two had an affair and keeping it from me, right? Then, I came up with the perfect case for why I could not have been the killer. I was there when the other two were murdered. I had a stab wound, and the best part? I couldn't remember a single thing! Why would I run if I were the killer? No one would have suspected that I was the one who did it. Then, the plot thickened, the engagement.

ring…that the police found where we dragged James' body could have worked, but we switched out the rings for a bigger size, so it looked like it just slipped off. When I removed my gloves while holding James' body, it fell off.

It all fell into place when I found the knife that I had hidden under the floorboards. You see, cops try to finish their jobs as soon as possible, so they only look at where the murders occurred, and if no item was found, they go off of what they have. There was a little hiccup when I found it, but I took care of him. The officer assisted with the plan when he killed Dustin, as Dustin had begun to reveal I was involved in the murders. The only way Dustin knew of my involvement was because he was semi-conscious as we dragged his and Alina's body into the forest, discussing our next steps. Anyway, once I had the murder weapon, we were able to change the course of this story.

I made it as if you called me up to the cabin to finish the job because I had found out what you did. After I stabbed you and you fell unconscious, back at the cabin, I placed it in.

your hands to get all the handprints needed. It made it look like you came to attack me because I found out the truth. The cops handled the rest of the puzzle. I had them revisit the crime scene, and, to their surprise, they found traces of your DNA. They discovered it in the carpet and near the fire pit where we burned all the sheets and bloody clothes. This was all thanks to a helpful and trustworthy friend, Officer Sam Carter. I had everything to carry out the perfect assassination without taking the fall. And that, Ethan, is how you get away with murder.

I know you always loved me, and I always loved you too. But you just screwed up a little too much. Maybe it was a mistake to save me.

You are probably thinking you'll show your lawyer this, and this will take me down. Well, I am sorry to burst your bubble. Your lawyer, Aiden Newman, is a personal close friend of mine and is serving his sentence for killing Dustin. If you try anything "smart", it will only backfire and make things worse for you as you spend your time in jail.

I wish you well, and I hope you can do the same for me, even if you can never forgive me.

Love you always,

Bailey C. XOXO

P.S. Enclosed is my favourite picture of us and the key necklace.

Present Day: January 1st, 2020

I stared at the cabin one last time. The only thing that I knew was what had happened within it. If only the walls had ears, as

Ethan had said. The horn honked loudly. I took one last big breath and said, "It's time to begin again", before walking away from Sugarbush Cabin, *Cabin 7*. I got into the car to hear the voice that made me feel safe. "Happy New Year, Mrs. Bailey Grayson."

"I like the sound of that, Mr. Sam Grayson." And with that being said, we hit the gas and drove off to a place where no one knew our names and story. The secret of the sugarbush murders stayed between us and the forest.

THE END

www.ingramcontent.com/pod-product-compliance
Lightning Source LLC
Chambersburg PA
CBHW040840010826
48978CB00012BB/840